Illustrated by Art Mawhinney and Meg Roldan
Adapted by Erin Rose Wage

Published by Phoenix International Publications, Inc.
8501 West Higgins Road   59 Gloucester Place
Chicago, Illinois 60631   London W1U 8JJ

we make books come alive is a trademark of Phoenix International Publications, Inc.

p i kids is a trademark of Phoenix International Publications, Inc.,
and is registered in the United States.
Look and Find is a trademark of
Phoenix International Publications, Inc.,
and is registered in the United States and Canada.

www.pikidsmedia.com

Printed in Canada.

8 7 6 5 4 3 2 1

ISBN: 978-1-5037-3378-7

SOLO
A STAR WARS STORY™

we make books come alive™

pi kids

Phoenix International Publications, Inc.

Chicago • London • New York • Hamburg • Mexico City • Paris • Sydney

Han's done it this time. He botched a very big heist he was working for the leader of the White Worms, Lady Proxima, and she has decided to make an example of him. Never one to go down without a fight, Han tries to bluff his way out. Qi'ra, on the other hand, is prepared to run.

Stay away from these troublemakers who want to stop Han and Qi'ra:

this scrumrat

this scrumrat

Rebolt

this enforcer

this scrumrat

Moloch

Lady Proxima

This Corellian M-68 landspeeder can really move—which is a good thing when you're being tailed by Imperials, White Worms, and a big, angry Grindalid (and his big, angry hounds). Han has gotten out of tight spots before with his speeder-piloting skills. Qi'ra hopes he can do it again.

While Qi'ra thinks about the odds, watch out for these speeders that are caught in the chase:

Moloch can't keep up with Han and Qi'ra in a foot chase. But Rebolt and Moloch's hounds can. Han and Qi'ra will have to hurry!

Find these fragrant things Han and Qi'ra can run past to confuse the hounds:

perfume

spices

livestock

barrel of eels

trash can

hot food

Right now seems like a good time for Han and Qi'ra to start a new life, far, far away from Corellia, the White Worms, and the Empire. Standing in line at the Coronet Spaceport, they anxiously try to blend in before they make their escape.

Han and Qi'ra are trying to walk casual. Lend them a hand by distracting these stormtroopers:

   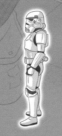   

The planet Mimban is covered in mud—the kind that can really weigh you down. As an Imperial mudtrooper, Han sees that the Empire is the enemy invader, not the native Mimbanese. He wants out.

As Han comes face-to-face with Tobias Beckett, search for these mud-covered things:

AT-hauler

goggles

"the beast"

blaster rifle

comlink

mudtrooper helmet

boot

glove

Han and Chewbacca are learning to work together...in the middle of a conveyex heist. Along with Beckett, Val, and Rio, they're attempting to separate one of the cars and carry it off with an AT-hauler. But Enfys Nest and the gang are getting in the way.

On the count of three, find Enfys and these Cloud-Riders:

Lando Calrissian is a notorious high-stakes sabacc player and the proud owner of the fastest ship in the galaxy, the *Millennium Falcon*. Beckett's crew needs a fast ship for their next heist. So Han is trying his luck against the smooth and sophisticated sportsman.

While Han tries to get Lando to bet his ship, survey the room for these ruffians, pirates, and players:

furry onlooker

Six Eyes

snug-necked
smuggler

the Twins

Lando Calrissian

wide-eyed
pirate

cloaked
spectator

hooded
beholder

The interior of the *Millennium Falcon* is as shiny as a Coruscant skyscraper. Lando and L3-37 give their new partners a tour of the ship. Han is certain that they can pull off the heist with this freighter.

Look around for some personal effects before Lando has any reason to worry that the *Falcon* won't be returned in perfect condition...

this flashy cape

plush pillow

this sporty cape

these stylish boots

carafe

sabacc cards

chrome-plated blaster

holochess pieces

Grindalids, like Lady Proxima and Moloch, are very sensitive to light, which is why they tend to dwell in dark, dank lairs. Return to the White Worms' den and spot this protective equipment:

Corellia used to manufacture some of the galaxy's best ships and speeders. Speed back to the chase and check out these parts and accessories:

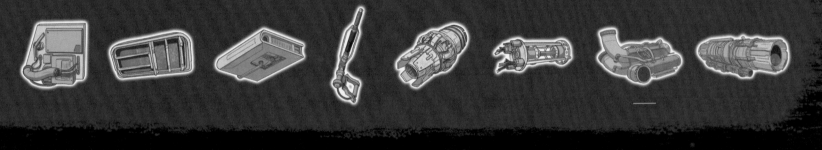

The Corellian market that Han and Qi'ra run through is full of unique things being sold or traded. Run back and browse these vendors' wares:

flustered
fish handler | spacey seller | aghast
eel slinger | preoccupied
peddler | frightened
fruit monger | shocked
shopkeeper | slop bucket
starer | vulnerable vendor

Han and Qi'ra aren't the only Corellians leaving their old lives behind. Get in line at the spaceport and find these other emigrants:

tunicked traveler | dark drifter | bearded rambler | emigrant from
another atmosphere | jolly jet-setter | wondering
wanderer | stoic sightseer

Knowing the mucky terrain inside and out gives the Mimbanese an advantage over the Imperial invaders. Trudge back to Mimban and see if you can locate these muddy Mimbanese:

Walking on the outside of a moving conveyex without proper magnetic footwear is risky, but that won't stop Beckett and his crew! Ride back to the heist and eye the boots on these range troopers:

Feeling lucky? Shuffle back to the sabacc game and flip over these cards and other gaming pieces:

this credit | these sabacc cards | this cup | gambling stake (reptilian epidermis) | these tokens | gambling stake (greel tree seedling) | gambling stake (chak-root) | this die

Even though this is the first time aboard for Beckett's crew, the *Falcon* feels like home. Blast back to the beloved light freighter and tidy up their things:

Qi'ra's blaster | Han's dice | Qi'ra's gloves | Chewie's goggles | Beckett's blaster | Beckett's backpack | Chewie's bandolier | Han's blaster